THIS

SWEET PICKLES ®

BOOK BELONGS TO

Michelle S.

In the world of *Sweet Pickles,* each animal gets into a pickle because of an all too human personality trait.

This book is about Zany Zebra. He's not afraid to be different, which really annoys Alligator, Dog and Kangaroo.

Other Books in the Sweet Pickles Series

ME TOO IGUANA
STORK SPILLS THE BEANS
GOOSE GOOFS OFF
VERY WORRIED WALRUS
FIXED BY CAMEL

Library of Congress Cataloging in Publication Data

Hefter, Richard.
  Zebra zips by.

  (Sweet Pickles series)
  SUMMARY : Zebra annoys the residents of Sweet Pickles
with his unconventional behavior.
  [1. Zebras–Fiction] I. Title. II. Series.
PZ7.H3587Ze   [E]   76-44019
ISBN 0-03-018081-3

Printed in the United States of America

Weekly Reader Books' Edition

Weekly Reader Books presents

ZIP GOES
ZEBRA

Written and Illustrated
by Richard Hefter
Edited by Ruth Lerner Perle

Holt, Rinehart and Winston · New York

Zebra went zipping by one day.
"Haw, haw!" laughed Kangaroo. "He's upside down!"

"He's really peculiar," muttered Alligator. "The other day he was eating dinner on a blanket under the table!"

"Yes!" shouted Kangaroo. "And he was eating his dessert first and his soup last. And when I asked him, 'Why?' he said, 'Why not?'"

"He does everything wrong," said Alligator. "It's outrageous! He takes showers in the car wash and his socks never match!"

"He's goofy," said Kangaroo.

"He's weird," said Dog.

"He's a menace," said Alligator.

"Look out!" shrieked Kangaroo. "Here he comes again!"

This time Zebra was riding a unicycle and standing on his head. And he was going backwards and he was singing.

"Did you see that!" giggled Kangaroo.

"See it?" yelled Alligator. "He almost rolled over my tail!"

"Aw, maybe he's only kidding," said Kangaroo.

"I doubt it," said Dog. "He's just weird."

"This has gone far enough," scowled Alligator. "We have to stop him."

They all marched down to Zebra's house.

When they got there, Alligator knocked on the door.
A voice from inside called, "Come on in, the window's open."

They climbed in the window.
"I thought so," grumbled Dog. "He's weird."

When they were all inside, Alligator said, "We want to know why you do everything wrong."
"What's wrong?" asked Zebra.

"Well," said Alligator, "you ride backwards and you eat under the table and you shower in the car wash and you wear a tie on your tail and you make us climb through your window and your socks don't match."

"And furthermore, you're making trouble," accused Alligator.

"Why?" asked Zebra. "I do things because they make me feel good. I ride backwards because I like to see where I've been, and a tie on my tail makes me feel dressed up, and the window is more fun than the door. Why should that bother you anyway? So, goodbye!"

Zebra threw them a kiss and galloped off.

"I didn't think it would work," said Dog.

"I have a plan," said Alligator. "Let's all do silly things. That'll teach him a lesson!"

Kangaroo painted dots on his nose and stuck a carrot in his ear.

Alligator tied a knot in her tail and puffed out her cheeks.

Dog put his pants on his head and his shirt on his legs.

They went out and stood on the
corner waiting for Zebra.

"Quick!" said Dog. "Here he comes!"
Kangaroo stood on his head.
Alligator crossed her eyes.
Dog made a funny face and said,
"BIPPYDIPPYDOOPLEDOOOP."

Zebra walked right by. He smiled and said, "Hello, Kangaroo. Hello, Alligator. Hello, Dog.

"Having fun?"

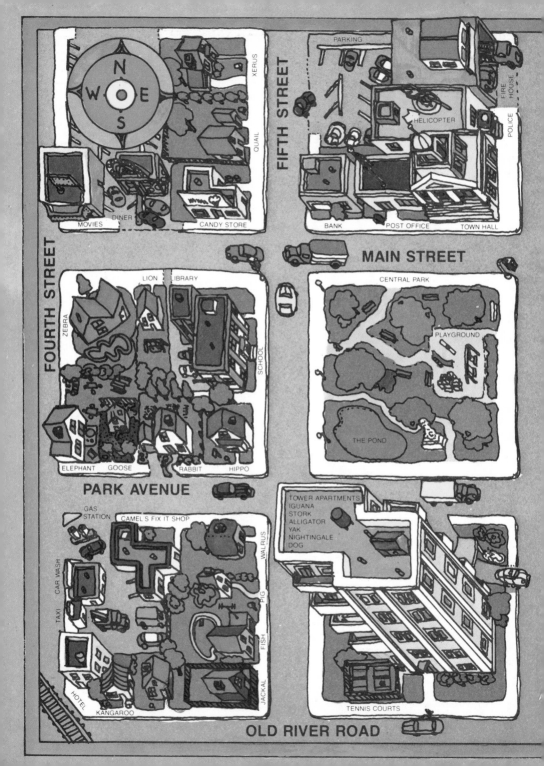